Note to parents, carers and teachers

Read it yourself is a series of modern stories, favourite characters and traditional tales written in a simple way for children who are learning to read. The books can be read independently or as part of a guided reading session.

Each book is carefully structured to include many high-frequency words vital for first reading. The sentences on each page are supported closely by pictures to help with understanding, and to offer lively details to talk about.

The books are graded into four levels that progressively introduce wider vocabulary and longer stories as a reader's ability and confidence grows.

Ideas for use

- Begin by looking through the book and talking about the pictures. Has your child heard this story before?

- Help your child with any words he does not know, either by helping him to sound them out or supplying them yourself.

- Developing readers can be concentrating so hard on the words that they sometimes don't fully grasp the meaning of what they're reading. Answering the puzzle questions at the end of the book will help with understanding.

For more information and advice on Read it yourself and book banding, visit www.ladybird.com/readityourself

Book Band 5

Level 1 is ideal for children who have received some initial reading instruction. Each story is told very simply, using a small number of frequently repeated words.

Special features:

Peter Rabbit

Old Brown

Benjamin

raft

Lily

nut

book

Squirrel Nutkin

Opening pages introduce key story words

6

7

Large, clear type

"We have to get to the island," said Benjamin.

"I can help!" said Squirrel Nutkin. "Jump on this raft."

Careful match between story and pictures

12

13

Educational Consultant: Geraldine Taylor
Book Banding Consultant: Kate Ruttle

LADYBIRD BOOKS

UK | USA | Canada | Ireland | Australia
India | New Zealand | South Africa

Ladybird Books is part of the Penguin Random House group of companies
whose addresses can be found at global.penguinrandomhouse.com.

ladybird.com

Penguin
Random House
UK

Text adapted from Peter's Secret Mission, first published by Puffin Books, 2014.
This version first published by Ladybird Books, 2015.
001

Printed in China

A CIP catalogue record for this book is available from the British Library
ISBN: 978-0-723-29521-1

Island Adventure

Based on the Peter Rabbit™
TV series

Peter Rabbit

Benjamin

Lily

nut

Old Brown

raft

book

Squirrel Nutkin

Peter Rabbit was looking for his dad's book.

"It is not here," he said. "Old Brown has taken it!"

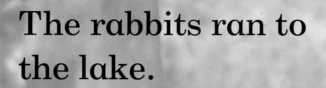

The rabbits ran to
the lake.

Old Brown was on the
island in the lake.

"We have to get to the island," said Benjamin.

"I can help!" said Squirrel Nutkin. "Jump on this raft."

13

The rabbits got to the island.

Peter saw Old Brown up
in his tree.

"We have to get the book
back," said Benjamin.

"I can help!" said Nutkin.

Up, up, up the tree he went.

17

"Here it is!" said Nutkin.
He had the book.

"You did it!" said Peter.

Just then, Old Brown
saw Nutkin!

Peter jumped up into the tree.

"Get off him!" Peter said.

"You can have Nutkin OR the book," said Old Brown.

"I will take Nutkin," said Peter. "Off we go!"

Whee!

Peter and Nutkin jumped, and Nutkin ran off.

The rabbits ran to
the lake.

"Get back on the raft,"
said Lily.

Just then, Nutkin ran up.
He had the book!

Old Brown was looking
for Nutkin.

"Take this nut, Peter!"
said Benjamin.

The nut went whee!

"Got him!" said Peter.

"We did it!" said Peter.
"We got Nutkin AND we
got Dad's book back!"

How much do you remember about the story of Peter Rabbit: Island Adventure? Answer these questions and find out!

- Who has taken the book from Peter?

- Where does Squirrel Nutkin find the book?

- What does Peter throw at Old Brown?

Look at the pictures from the story and say the order they should go in.

A

B

C

D

Answer: B, C, A, D.

Tick the books you've read!

Level 1

Level 2